Santa's Song

A playful holiday sing-along song for children of all ages

Pamela McColl

GRAFTON & SCRATCH
PUBLISHERS

Nearly everyone knows

the words and tune of the holiday carol "We Wish You A Merry Christmas and a Happy New Year". Here is the giggly way dearest Santa sings the song as he rides by sleigh through the skies on Christmas Eve. Santa loves to sing-along as he brings joy to boys and girls all over the world. Maybe you are one of the children Santa has on his list and your house is one of the homes he visits on the most special night!

Santa's reindeer friends are very good at singing the song this special alphabetic way. They love to throw letters to each other as they pull Santa's sleigh. If you practise you too will be singing along very soon! Can you guess who it is at the North Pole that sings this song the best of all?

Turn the page to and you will find out who it is!

Here is the answer:

**The elves sing this silly
song the best of all!**

They call it The Elfabetic Singing Game!

Elves love to have fun, to sing and to make toys,
and of course eat gum drops. Elves also love to
play around and spell words in funny ways.

"Ho Ho Ho! Happy Christmas To All!"

Or as the elves like to say,

"Ho Ho Ho—Happy Hristmas To Hall!"

How to play and sing Santa's Song

(an alphabet singing game)

Add new words to the traditional tune to create a fun sing–song game that plays with letters of the alphabet. You can go from the letter "B" all the way straight through to "Z" or pick any letter and start there first.

Some of the letters are especially fun and you will soon have your own favorites. You can also play around with fun letter combinations. After you have practised with the letters ask your

friends or family to join in. Play it as a game and
ask people to suggest a letter from this list and
then let the fun begin.

Here are the letters to choose from:

B C D F G H J K L M N P R S T V W Y Z

We left off Q and A E I O U because they are just
too silly for words!

The popular holiday song "We Wish You a Merry Christmas" is very, very, very old. Some people say it was written over 500 years ago in jolly old England. It has been the custom for hundreds of years for people to sing this song, along with other charming songs such as "Jingle Bells" and "Deck the Halls", as they go from house to house caroling at Christmas time.

Caroling or singing to spread good cheer was often rewarded with a yummy treat as a thank-you for the merry making shared through song. You may want to go out caroling this holiday season with your friends. Today people go caroling to raise funds for good causes and the tradition continues.

We wish you a mer-ry Christ-mas, we wish you a mer-ry

Christ-mas, we wish you a mer-ry Christ-mas and a hap - py New

Year! Good tid-ings we bring to you and your kin; Good

tid - ings for Christ-mas and a hap - py New Year! We

wish you a mer-ry Christ-mas, we wish you a mer-ry Christ-mas, we

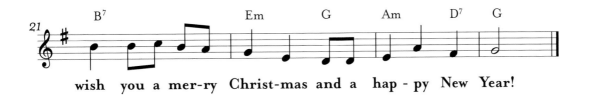

wish you a mer-ry Christ-mas and a hap - py New Year!

You may want to sing the song a few times with the original words to practise the melody. Here are the words to the song:

We wish you a merry Christmas
We wish you a merry Christmas
We wish you a merry Christmas
and a happy New Year.

Good tidings we bring
To you and your kin,
We wish you a merry Christmas
And a happy New Year!

Now bring us some figgy pudding,
Now bring us some figgy pudding,
Now bring us some figgy pudding,
Now bring us some here.

We won't go until we get it,
We won't go until we get it,
We won't go until we get it,
So bring some right here.

We all like our figgy pudding,
We all like our figgy pudding,
So bring us some figgy pudding,
With all its good cheer!

We wish you a merry Christmas
We wish you a merry Christmas
We wish you a merry Christmas
And a happy New Year!

Now for the new version starting with the letter B, turn the page!

Be bish bou a berry Bhristmas
Be bish bou a berry Bhristmas
Be bish bou a berry Bhristmas
And a babby Bew Bear!

Good tidings we bring to you and your kin,
We wish you a merry Christmas
And a happy New Year!

Ce cish cou a cerry Christmas
Ce cish cou a cerry Christmas
Ce cish cou a cerry Christmas
And a cappy Cew Cear!

Good tidings we bring to you and your kin,
We wish you a merry Christmas
And a happy New Year!

De dish dou a derry Dhristmas
De dish dou a derry Dhristmas
De dish dou a derry Dhristmas
And a dabby Dew Dear!

Good tidings we bring to you and your kin,
We wish you a merry Christmas
And a happy New Year!

Fe fish fou a ferry Fhristmas
Fe fish fou a ferry Fhristmas
Fe fish fou a ferry Fhristmas
And a fabby Few Fear!

Good tidings we bring to you and your kin,
We wish you a merry Christmas
And a happy New Year!

Ge gish gou a gerry Ghristmas
Ge gish gou a gerry Ghristmas
Ge gish gou a gerry Ghristmas
And a gabby Gew Gear!

Good tidings we bring to you and your kin,
We wish you a merry Christmas
And a happy New Year!

He hish hou a herry Hristmas
He hish hou a herry Hristmas
He hish hou a herry Hristmas
And a habby Hew Hear!

Good tidings we bring to you and your kin,
We wish you a merry Christmas
And a happy New Year!

Je jish jou a jerry Jhristmas
Je jish jou a Jerry Jhristmas
Je jish jou a Jerry Jhristmas
And a jabby Jew Jear!

Good tidings we bring to you and your kin,
We wish you a merry Christmas
And a happy New Year!

Ke kish kou a kerry Khristmas
Ke kish kou a kerry Khristmas
Ke kish kou a kerry Khristmas
And a kabby Kew Kear!

Good tidings we bring to you and your kin,
We wish you a merry Christmas
And a happy New Year!

Le lish lou a lerry Lhristmas
Le lish lou a lerry Lhristmas
Le lish lou a lerry Lhristmas
And a labby Lew Lear!

Good tidings we bring to you and your kin,
We wish you a merry Christmas
And a happy New Year!

Me mish mou a merry Mhristmas
Me mish mou a merry Mhristmas
Me mish mou a merry Mhristmas
And a mabby Mew Mear!

Good tidings we bring to you and your kin,
We wish you a merry Christmas
And a happy New Year!

Ne nish nou a nerry Nhristmas
Ne nish nou a nerry Nhristmas
Ne nish nou a nerry Nhristmas
And a nabby New Near!

Good tidings we bring to you and your kin,
We wish you a merry Christmas
And a happy New Year!

Pe pish pou a perry Phristmas
Pe pish pou a perry Phristmas
Pe pish pou a perry Phristmas
And a pabby Pew Pear!

Good tidings we bring to you and your kin,
We wish you a merry Christmas
And a happy New Year!

Re rish rou a rerry Rhristmas
Re rish rou a rerry Rhristmas
Re rish rou a rerry Rhristmas
And a rabby Rew Rear!

Good tidings we bring to you and your kin,
We wish you a merry Christmas
And a happy New Year!

Se sish sou a serry Shristmas
Se sish sou a serry Shristmas
Se sish sou a serry Shristmas
And a sabby Sew Sear!

Good tidings we bring to you and your kin,
We wish you a merry Christmas
And a happy New Year!

Te tish tou a terry Thristmas
Te tish tou a terry Thristmas
Te tish tou a terry Thristmas
And a tabby Tew Tear!

Good tidings we bring to you and your kin,
We wish you a merry Christmas
And a happy New Year!

Ve vish vou a verry Vhristmas
Ve vish vou a verry Vhristmas
Ve vish vou a verry Vhristmas
And a vabby Vew Vear!

Good tidings we bring to you and your kin,
We wish you a merry Christmas
And a happy New Year!

We wish wou a werry Whristmas
We wish wou a werry Whristmas
We wish wou a werry Whristmas
And a wabby Wew Wear!

Good tidings we bring to you and your kin,
We wish you a merry Christmas
And a happy New Year!

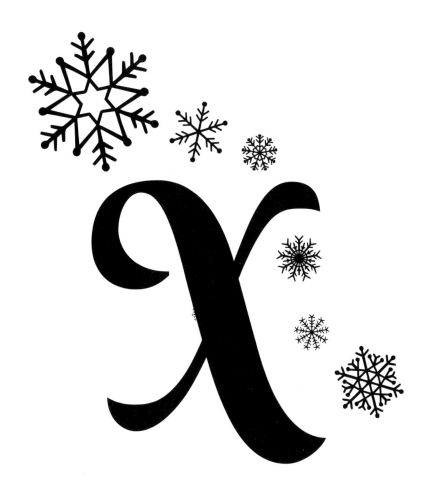

Xe xish xou a xerry Xhristmas
Xe xish xou a xerry Xhristmas
Xe xish xou a xerry Xhristmas
and a xappy Xew Xear!

Good tidings we bring to you and your kin,
We wish you a merry Christmas
And a happy New Year!

Ye yish you a yerry Yhristmas
Ye yish you a yerry Yhristmas
Ye yish you a yerry Yhristmas
and a yappy Yew Year!

Good tidings we bring to you and your kin,
We wish you a merry Christmas
And a happy New Year!

3

Ze zish zou a zerry Zhristmas
Ze zish zou a zerry Zhristmas
Ze zish zou a zerry Zhristmas
And a zabby Zew Zear!

Good tidings we bring to you and your kin,
We wish you a merry Christmas
And a happy New Year!

Did you notice Santa's reindeer in our cover?
That is Dasher!

We have produced a darling plush reindeer, *Dasher The Reindeer Doll*,
to go along with *Santa's Song* and *Twas The Night Before Christmas*
created by Merrymakers USA.
Dasher is available by special order through the publisher
at graftonandscratch@gmail.com. Supplies limited.

Follow *Santa's Song* on Facebook.

Published in the USA and in Canada in 2017 by GRAFTON & SCRATCH PUBLISHERS
www.graftonandscratch.com
Distributed by Atlas Books/Bookmasters Ohio, USA

Book design by Elisa Gutiérrez

The text is set in *Mrs. Eaves*, and *Wreath* for the title and ornaments

Printed in the US   10 9 8 7 6 5 4 3 2 1

LIBRARY AND ARCHIVES CANADA CATALOGUING IN PUBLICATION

McColl, Pamela, 1958-, author
Santa's song : a playful sing-along song for children of all ages / Pamela
McColl.

Issued in print and electronic formats.
ISBN 978-1-927979-23-5 (hardcover).--ISBN 978-1-927979-24-2 (HTML).--
ISBN 978-1-927979-25-9 (PDF)

1. Christmas music--Texts--Juvenile literature. 2. Songs, English--Texts.
I. Title.
M1998.M129 2017   j782.42026'8   C2017-902706-9
                                                C2017-902707-7